Better Homes and Gardens®

Dandy Dragon Day

"Careful," Max said. "This is the biggest card house we've ever made."

Sara Jo added another card. "I know. This one makes twenty-six."

Suddenly, Max's little sister, Marci, burst into the room. "Guess what day this is!"

Sara Jo's hand jerked. The card house quivered, but it didn't fall.

"Sh-h-h, Marci. We can't build this with you making so much noise," Max said.

"But this is *important!*" Marci insisted.

"Go away! Come back when we're done."

Marci looked sadly at Max and left.

"My turn," said Max. He took a deep breath. His hand shook as he balanced the card. "I hope *I* don't knock it down. Twenty-..."

Just then Marci ran back into the room with a banner flying behind her. "Max, look what I found! Our old party banner, remember?"

A big whoosh of air followed Marci.

The card house started to collapse. Sara Jo reached out to stop it, but it fell, scattering the cards in all directions. "Oh, no! You wrecked our house."

"Marci, cut it out!" Max shouted.

Marci dropped the banner. "It's Dandy Dragon Day, and you don't even care." She ran from the room crying.

Max picked up the banner. "I forgot that today is Dandy Dragon Day. When we lived in Dragontown, everybody celebrated it."

"I never heard of it," said Sara Jo.

Max's face lit up. "Oh, it can be lots of fun. My mom and dad say it's a day when dragons remember that *everyone* is special. And, it's best when we invite friends over for a big party. I know! Let's have a surprise Dandy Dragon Day party for Marci. That should make her feel much better."

So they ran to the willow tree to make plans for the party.

"Hey, what's that?" Vera asked.

"It's a banner for Dandy Dragon Day, the best holiday of the year. We're going to have a party," said Max.

Vera tossed one long ear over her shoulder. "Don't be silly. Beautiful Bunny Day is the best holiday of the year. But . . . I do love parties."

"Weird Weasel Day is the best holiday," Gus said. "But I'll come to your party if you're having food."

Max grinned. "We're going to have lots of food. But let's decorate first. Everyone draw some dragon pictures."

Elliot looked over Vera's shoulder. "Dragons don't have long fuzzy ears."

"*My* dragons do," Vera said, coloring the inside of her dragon ears pink.

Gus and Arnie took turns hanging up the dragon pictures.

"They look great," Max said. "Let's go find Marci so we can start our party. Everybody yell 'surprise' when we bring her back."

Max and Sara Jo looked in Marci's room,
but she wasn't there. "She must be around
here somewhere," Sara Jo said. "Let's keep
looking."

They searched and searched, but couldn't
find Marci. "Max, where could she be?" Sara
Jo asked. "We have looked everywhere."

"I feel awful," said Max. "Marci's gone, and
it's all my fault."

Just then Max looked down and saw a
small dragon's tail sticking out from under
the bushes. He peeked through the bushes
and found Marci with a pile of cards.

"Marci, what are you doing?" asked Max.

"I was trying to build you the biggest card house ever, so you wouldn't be mad at me. But I couldn't."

Max smiled. "Oh, I'm not mad."

"Sara Jo is mad." Marci sniffled.

Sara Jo stuck her head under the bush.

"No, I'm not. Not anymore."

Max took Marci's hand. "Come on. We have something to show you." Max and Sara Jo led Marci back to the willow tree.

"*SURPRISE!*" everybody
yelled when they saw Marci.
"Happy Dandy Dragon Day,"
Max said.

"A party for me?" asked Marci.
"Uh-huh. And everyone
helped make the decorations."

"Hey, I'm *very* hungry," Gus said.

"Me, too," said Max. "Let's go make some sandwiches."

Max set up an assembly line at the table, and everybody pitched in to help.

"Arnie is eating all the pickles," Tweetums screeched.

"I am not," said Arnie, talking with his mouth full.

When the sandwiches were ready, they all sat at the table and dug in.

"Wow, these taste great!" said Gus. "They're even better than my mom's Weird Weasel Waffles."

Vera daintily wiped her mouth with a napkin. "They're not as delicious as Beautiful Bunny Buns, but they are yummy."

Max stood up. "Let's go outside and play some dragon games."

"Oh, boy!" Sara Jo said, heading for the door.

"Wait," Marci said. "You don't go through the door that way on Dandy Dragon Day."

"Why not?"

"You have to do it like this." Marci backed through the door and said "Dandy Dragon Day" three times, as fast as she could.

Tweetums giggled. "That looks like fun."

"Me next," said Elliot.

"No, me!" said Ozzy hurrying to get in line.

"OK," Max said, "it's game time."
They all spent the afternoon playing Dipsy
Dragon, Dragon Dribble, and Dunk the
Dragon.

What you'll need...

- 1 plastic-foam or paper cup, or one 4½-inch cardboard tube (toilet paper tube)
- Crafts knife or small, sharp knife
- Thin strips of crepe paper or tissue paper
- Tape
- 1 crafts stick or unsharpened pencil
- White crafts glue
- 2 buttons
- 2 cotton balls

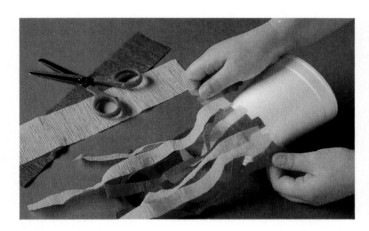

1 Have an adult cut out the bottom of the cup. Place several strips of crepe paper side by side so they touch. Cut a piece of tape that's longer than the width of all the crepe paper strips. Lay the tape across the top of the strips. Stick the tape with the crepe paper near the bottom edge of the cup (see photo).

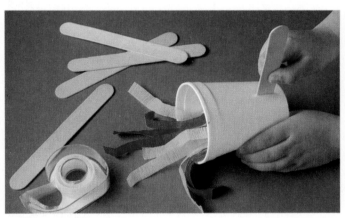

2 Push the crepe paper strips through the cup. With adult help, cut a slit in the cup on the side opposite the crepe paper strips. Gently push the crafts stick into the slit (see photo). If necessary, use tape to hold the stick to the cup.

3 For the eyes, glue one button on each cotton ball. Glue the eyes to the cup (see photo). Also, see Dragon Faces on page 32.

To make your dragon breathe "fire," hold the cup up to your mouth and blow through the end near the stick.

Dandy Dragon

An egg carton is the perfect dragon body—it comes complete with bumps.

What you'll need...

- Markers, crayons, or paint
- 1 cardboard egg carton, lid and flap removed
- Scissors
- Construction paper
- Two 4½-inch cardboard tubes (toilet paper tubes)
- Tape or white crafts glue

1 For the dragon's body, use markers to decorate the egg carton any way you like (see photo).

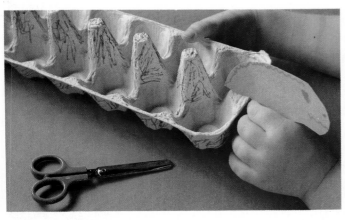

2 Cut a small slit (about ½ inch long) in each end of the egg carton. Cut a dragon's head and tail out of construction paper. Fold over the end of the head and tail so you have a double thickness of paper. Push the double thickness of the head into 1 slit and the tail into the other slit (see photo).

3 For the dragon's legs, cut each cardboard tube in half. Decorate the legs any way you like. Push one leg over each corner egg cup (see photo). Tape in place. If desired, cut feet out of construction paper. Tape to the bottom of the legs.

Sleeping Dragon Sandwiches

A toasty bed with a cheesy blanket is a fine place for dragons to nap.

What you'll need...

- Bread slices, toasted and halved, or melba toast slices
- Baking sheet

- Frankfurters, sliced, or pimiento-stuffed olives or dill pickles, halved lengthwise

- American or process Swiss cheese slices, halved
- Chow mein noodles (optional)

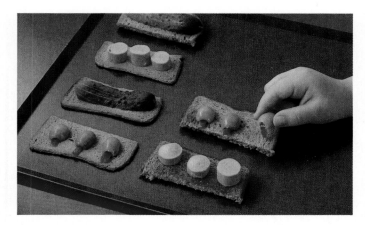

1 Place toasted bread halves on a baking sheet. For the dragons, arrange 3 frankfurter pieces, 3 olive halves, or 1 pickle half on each piece of toast (see photo).

2 For a blanket, place a half-slice of cheese on top of the "dragons" resting on the toast (see photo). For the pickle dragon, fold back one corner of the cheese, if desired.

3 With adult help, broil the sandwiches about 4 inches from the heat for 1 to 3 minutes or till the cheese melts. Cool slightly.
   For the dragon's tail, stick a chow mein noodle under the cheese near each dragon, if desired (see photo).

Fire-Breathing Dragon

Dragon Faces: How do you make a dragon's face? Any way you want to! Buttons, cotton balls, beads, sequins, and corks turn into eyes and noses when glued or taped to the cup or the cardboard tube. Yarn, bottle tops, dried pasta, and dried cereal work, too.

The Fire-Breathing Dragon is fun to use as a puppet. For show time, sit behind a table or chair so the audience can't see you. Hold the puppet up above the edge of the table or chair so the audience can see the puppet. Make up a story about your dragon and tell it to the people watching. You can even make the dragon talk in a funny voice.

Dandy Dragon

Even though we used cardboard egg cartons, the plastic-foam egg cartons work, too. To decorate the foam cartons, glue pieces of paper or pretty beads to the carton to add color. Or, color the carton with permanent markers. (Be sure to ask for permission before you color with permanent markers.)

When your dragon is finished, use it to hold some of your extra-special fun stuff. Or, fill it with candy and give it to a friend for May Day or as a special gift. It's also a fun party decoration for the table.

A cardboard carton from a 6- or 8-pack of soda also can be used to carry your special belongings in. Decorate it with the same things you use for the egg carton.

When you're done decorating, pretend you're a doctor and use the carton as your doctor's kit. Or, you can be a carpenter and use it as your tool box. Do you know other people who carry things in a special bag?

Sleeping Dragon Sandwiches

Words that rhyme are fun to say while you play. Act out this silly rhyme while an adult reads it aloud to you.

Shhh . . . little dragons are
  sleeping sound.
So be very, very quiet—tip-
  toe around.

They're all covered up from
  their noses to their feet.
Snuggled in covers and
  blankets and sheets.

While asleep, they dream of
  dragony things.
Like long tails, green scales,
  and big dragon wings.

When they wake up, they'll
  be ready to play.
And start the celebration of
  Dandy Dragon Day.

BETTER HOMES AND GARDENS® BOOKS

Editor: Gerald M. Knox   Art Director: Ernest Shelton   Managing Editor: David A. Kirchner
Department Head, Family Life: Sharyl Heiken

DANDY DRAGON DAY

Editors: Jennifer Darling and Sandra Granseth   Graphic Designers: Brenda Lesch and Linda Vermie
Editorial Project Manager: Angela K. Renkoski
Contributing Writer: Jane Stanley   Contributing Illustrator: Buck Jones
Contributing Color Artist: Sue Fitzpatrick Cornelison   Contributing Photographer: Scott Little

Have BETTER HOMES AND GARDENS® magazine delivered to your door.
For information, write to: ROBERT AUSTIN, P.O. BOX 4536, DES MOINES, IA 50336